P9-DFI-380

Never Poke a Squid

Never Poke a Squid

Story and Pictures by

DENYS CAZET

ORCHARD BOOKS / NEW YORK

Orchard Books, A Grolier Company
95 Madison Avenue, New York, NY 10016

Manufactured in the United States of America
Printed and bound by Phoenix Color Corp.
Book design by Mina Greenstein
The text of this book is set in 16 point ITC Bookman Light.
The illustrations are watercolor paintings.

10 9 8 7 6 5 4 3 2 1

Library of Congress Cataloging-in-Publication Data
Cazet, Denys.
Never poke a squid / story and pictures by Denys Cazet.
p. cm.
Summary: Arnie and Raymond recount the Halloween celebration at school in which the principal accidentally got sprayed with a bag of ink.
ISBN 0-531-30279-2 (trade)—ISBN 0-531-33279-9 (library)
[1. Halloween—Fiction. 2. Schools—Fiction. 3. Friendship—Fiction.] I. Title.
PZ7.C2985 Nc 2000 [E]—dc21 99-54161

For Virginia Maurer,
poet, gardener, artist—
but, above all else,
Grandma
—D.C.

Arnie's mother looked out of the kitchen window.
A giant squid looked back.
Mother screamed.
"We're home!" said Arnie.

Mother helped Arnie and Raymond take off their costume. "How are you, Raymond?" she asked.
"It wasn't our fault," he said.
Mother poured some cold milk. "What do you mean?"
"Never poke a squid in the ink bag!" said Arnie.
"That's the Rule of the Sea," added Raymond.

Mother put some cookies on the table.
“Someone poked you?”
“Principal,” said Arnie.
“Accident!” said Raymond.
“Uh, oh!” said Mother.

Mother sat down at the table.
"Why don't you tell me all about it?" she said.

"Same old thing." Arnie shrugged. "First we say the Pledge to the pigeons. Then we count how many people want their lunch hot."

"And mark the calendar," added Raymond. "Today is Halloween."

?

I don't see any flag. Did someone take it?

I pledge allegiance to the flag of the United States of America, and to the Republic . . .
I pledge allegiance to the pigeon . . .
. . . of the United Stripes of America . . .
My mother's Pledge is lemon scented!
Your flag is lemon scented?
¿Su mamá es un limón?

Nuestra calabaza mide veinte pulgadas.
I dub thee Prince Pumpkin Lips.
You're supposed to count them, not eat them!
Ours is biggest!
Ouch!
Whoa! Mine is bigger!

What?
Inches or centimeters?
Ooops. Sorry!
HELP!

"Everyone got a pumpkin!" said Arnie.
"To take home?" Mother asked.
Raymond took a cookie. "Pumpkin math!"
"We weighed them on a scale," said Arnie.
"We used strings to see which one was the biggest."
"The teacher had a jar filled with candy corn. We tried to guesstimate," said Raymond.

"After recess we made trick-or-treat bags."

"We decorated cookies for the party," said Raymond. "These taste better."

"Thank you," said Mother.

"Everybody helped decorate the room," Arnie said. "Mrs. Hippowitz hung up her pineapple."

"Pineapple?"

"That thing with the candy in it."

"You mean piñata."

"Whatever," said Arnie.

OUR WORK
No, no, not on one! Wait until I count to three. Ready?
Er . . . Excuse me . . .
She said we could each make one cookie!
Okay, this one is mine.
This thing is stuck. Ooops!
What are you doing?
¡Escondiendo!

“Did Mrs. Hippowitz wear a costume?”
“Ballerina,” said Arnie.
“During music she played ‘Night on Bald Mountain.’ She showed us some fancy steps.”
Raymond put down his glass of milk. “She had to sit down for a while.”
“To rest?” asked Mother.
“There was a rip,” said Arnie.
“It was big,” said Raymond. “Really, really big.”
“I can imagine,” Mother gasped.

Whoa!
WHOA!
Let’s see—weight, plus height of projectile, plus tensile strength of material . . .
Do you hear music?
¿Has visto a la niña?
Don’t turn around!
?

RIPPP!
Whoa!
Whoa!
Bonk
Bonk
Bonk
Bonk
Bonk
Bonk
Pay attention!
Uh-oh!

Arnie bent over and tied his shoelace. "There was a lot of trouble at lunch."

Mother leaned forward. "Is this the part about the principal and the ink bag?"

Hmmmm . . . beanie weenies + one giant squid = a mess.

"No," said Arnie. "The teacher let us wear costumes at lunch."

"And . . .?"

"And you can't eat beanie weenies with suction cups."

"May I have another cookie?" Raymond asked.

"We're starving," said Arnie.

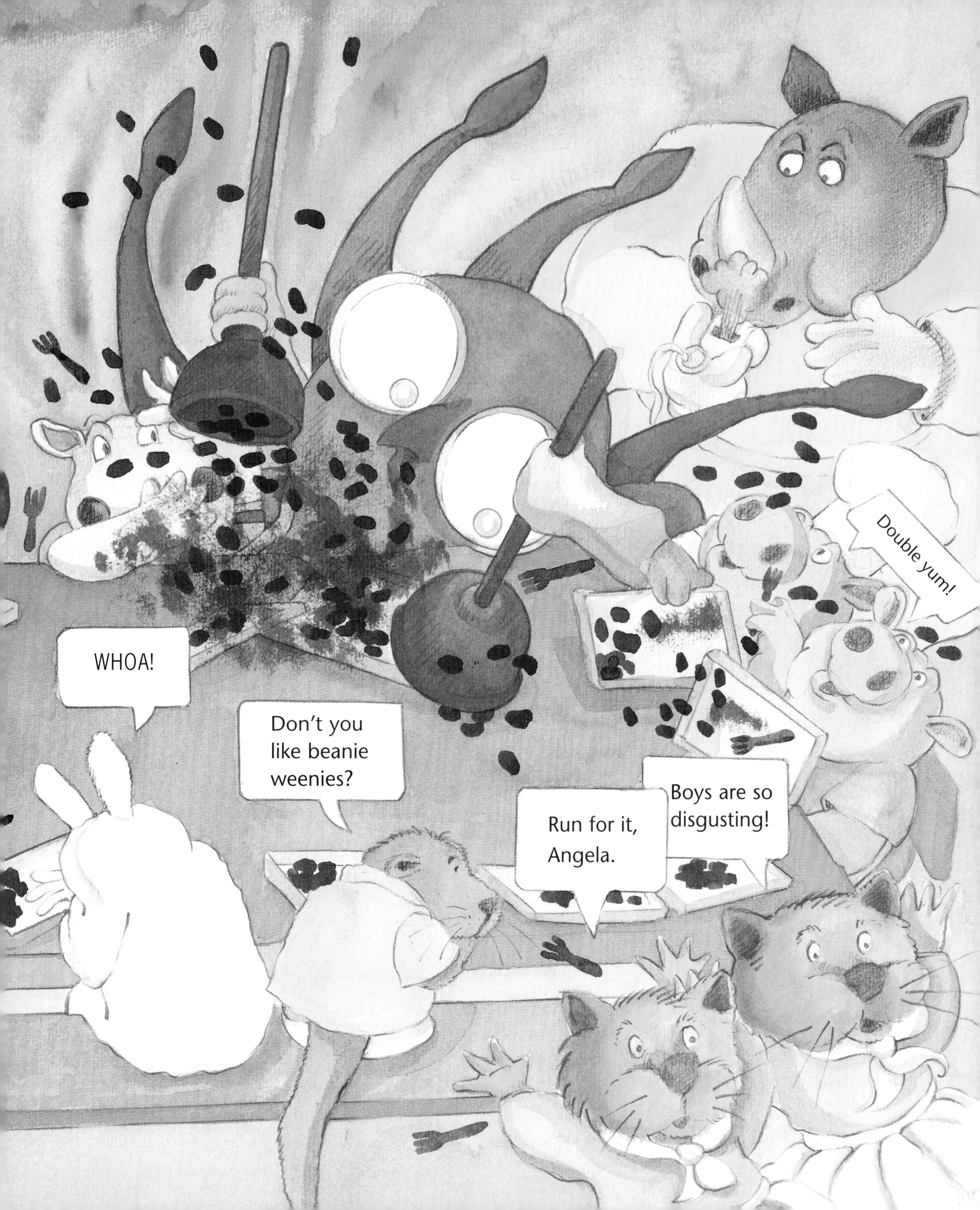
Double yum!
WHOA!
Don't you like beanie weenies?
Boys are so disgusting!
Run for it, Angela.

¡La cucaracha!
Isn't he wonderful? He called me "cucaracha"!
I said I wanted to be a mommy, not a mummy!
There goes my father's hat!
Oh.
?
Hey! Who put the onions in here?

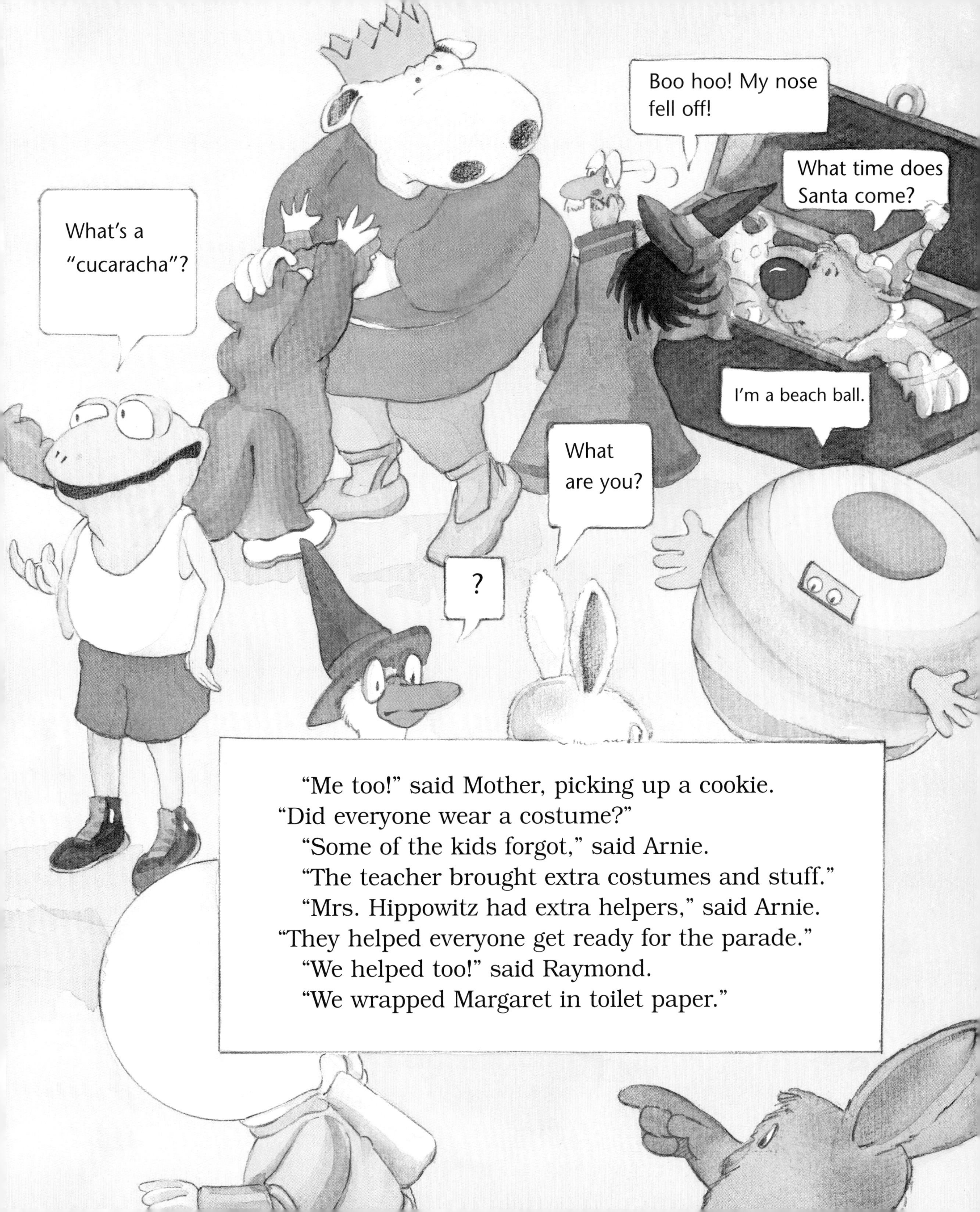

"Me too!" said Mother, picking up a cookie. "Did everyone wear a costume?"

"Some of the kids forgot," said Arnie.

"The teacher brought extra costumes and stuff."

"Mrs. Hippowitz had extra helpers," said Arnie. "They helped everyone get ready for the parade."

"We helped too!" said Raymond.

"We wrapped Margaret in toilet paper."

Mother filled the plate with more cookies. "And then . . ."

"Then we marched down Main Street," said Arnie.

Raymond ate another cookie. "It was a parade."

"It went smoothly?" Mother asked.

"I think so," said Arnie.

"Sort of," said Raymond.

Watch that pole!
What?
Ow!
Halloween crossing! Hold it!
Stop at the corner. . . . The corner! The corner!
My dad's not going to like this!
La cucaracha, La cucaracha . . .
He loves me, he loves me not, he loves me. . . .

"When we came back, we had a big party," said Arnie.
"We had an 'eat the donut' race."
"We played pin-the-wart-on-the-witch."
"Then . . . we whacked Mrs. Hippowitz's pineapple!"
"Piñata," said Mother.
"Whatever," said Arnie.
These would taste better without the strings.
Am I getting closer?
Uh-oh! Someone better call the police.
Mine.
Mine.

Attack of the giant squid!
A little to the left . . .
Mine.
Yum! Mine, mine!
Mine.
Yo quiero dulces.
I heard that! Now I'm his "dulces"!

Squid juice!
Squid juice!
Squid juice!
Squid juice!
Squid juice!
SQUID JUICE!
Squid juice!
Squid juice!
Squid juice!
Squid juice!
Squid juice!

"Are we to the part about the principal yet?"

"Yep!" said Arnie. "He read us a scary story and gave us awards."

"Awards?"

"I got the 'most improved' award."

"I got the 'best friend' award," said Raymond. "Arnie made it for me."

Arnie slid off his chair and put his arm around his mother. "Never poke a squid in the ink bag!" he said.

"That's the Rule of the Sea," added Raymond.

Mother sat back in her chair and smiled. "Just another day in the first grade," she said.

Arnie picked up his costume.

"It's not over!"

"No," said Raymond. "We still have to go trick-or-treating!"

"Maybe you should stay over," said Arnie.

"Raymond, would you like to stay over?" Mother asked.

Raymond looked at his shoes and nodded.

"We'd really like you to," she said gently.

"Nobody ever asked me before," said Raymond.

Mother picked up the phone. "I'll call your dad and see if it's okay."

"Hooray!" said Arnie. "Come on . . . let's refill the ink bag!"

Arnie ran up the stairs. Raymond stopped in the doorway. He looked at Arnie's mother. "I'm Arnie's friend," he said.

"Mine too," said Mother.

Lebanon Valley College
Bishop Library
Annville, PA 17003
GAYLORD RG